RAINBOW BOY

by **Taylor Rouanzion**

illustrated by **Stacey Chomiak**

beaming books

MINNEAPOLIS

For Noah, my very own rainbow kid.
—T.R.

For Robson and Hudson.
—S.C.

Text copyright © 2021 Taylor Rouanzion
Illustrations copyright © 2021 Stacey Chomiak

Published in 2021 by Beaming Books, an imprint of 1517 Media. All rights reserved.
No part of this book may be reproduced without the written permission of the publisher.
Email copyright@1517.media. Printed in Canada.

26 25 24 23 22 21   2 3 4 5 6 7 8 9

Hardcover ISBN: 978-1-5064-6398-8
Ebook ISBN: 978-1-5064-6661-3

Library of Congress Cataloging-in-Publication Data

Names: Rouanzion, Taylor, author. | Chomiak, Stacey, illustrator.
Title: Rainbow boy / by Taylor Rouanzion ; illustrated by Stacey Chomiak.
Description: Minneapolis, MN : Beaming Books, 2020. | Audience: Ages 3-8. |
   Summary: Unable to choose one favorite color, a young boy enjoys wearing
   a pink tutu on Sundays, playing with an orange basketball on Tuesdays,
   and trying to change things with a purple wand on Saturdays.
Identifiers: LCCN 2019056898 (print) | LCCN 2019056899 (ebook) | ISBN
   9781506463988 (hardcover) | ISBN 9781506466613 (ebook)
Subjects: CYAC: Color--Fiction. | Sex role--Fiction. | Family
   life--Fiction.
Classification: LCC PZ7.1.R765 Rai 2020 (print) | LCC PZ7.1.R765 (ebook)
   | DDC [E]--dc23
LC record available at https://lccn.loc.gov/2019056898
LC ebook record available at https://lccn.loc.gov/2019056899

65087; 9781506463988; JAN2021

Beaming Books
510 Marquette Avenue
Minneapolis, MN 55402
Beamingbooks.com

Grown-ups are always asking me,
"What's your favorite color?"

But with so many amazing colors,
how can I choose just one?
So this is what I say. . .

On Sundays, my favorite color is **pink**.

I put on my sparkly pink tutu
and shiny tiara and play ballerina.

I twirl and leap and balance on one foot.

I am the most graceful boy who has ever been.

On Mondays, my favorite color is red.

I find my best, sharpest red crayon and draw
row after row of red roses, with their swirly
centers and bright red petals.

When I'm finished, I give the best one to Mommy
and the other best one to Daddy.

On Tuesdays, my favorite color is orange.

I bounce my orange basketball all around the backyard.

Daddy says I'm not supposed to kick it, but I do anyway.
And when it lands right in Mommy's orange flower bed,
Daddy laughs and yells "Goal!" before fishing it out for me.

On Wednesdays, my favorite color is yellow.

I feed my baby doll yellow bananas and rub yellow lotion all over her so she's not itchy,

and then I put on her yellow pajamas.

I sing her a lullaby and lay her in a little crib, then whisper in her ear that she's the sweetest baby ever.

On Thursdays, my favorite color is green.

I wear a scaly green mermaid tail and spread out Mommy's favorite green quilt (shhh, don't tell!) and swim in an ocean of green until dinner.

Then I wash my fins and doggy-paddle to the table.

On Fridays, my favorite color is **blue**.

I use blue glitter and glue to make sparkly blue snowflakes, then I hang them in the window to dry.

In the afternoon, when the warm sun comes out, I pretend the snowflakes melt to the floor and make giant puddles I can splash in.

On Saturdays, my favorite color is **purple**.

I put on my silky purple cape and wield my star-shaped magic wand.

I run around the house shouting "PRESTO CHANGE-O!" at the dog to see if she'll turn into a rabbit.

"Can I really change things, Mommy?" I ask.

She kisses me on my magician's nose and says,
"You can change the world, my magic boy."

Sometimes, even after I've given grown-ups my WHOLE answer to their "favorite color" question, they will ask me, "But what if you could only choose one?"

I don't know what to say to that.

Thinking about choosing just one color makes me sad.

I love my pink tutu *and*
my orange basketball
and my green mermaid tail.

I couldn't possibly give any of them up!

But then Mommy hugs me close and whispers in my ear,

"It's okay. Your heart is just too big for one color alone.
You need a whole rainbow to fill it up.

Don't you, my rainbow boy?"

She's right, you know.

(See? This is my heart.)

About the author & illustrator

TAYLOR ROUANZION lives in Northern California with her husband, child, and miniature dachshund. She has been a part of local support groups for trans/gender-nonconforming kids and their parents. Her own child is gender nonconforming and has inspired Taylor to write for her and others like her so they can be seen in children's literature.

Taylor earned her bachelor's degree in English and is currently studying for her master's in library and information science. She has worked as a children's and youth library assistant and hopes to become a children's librarian someday in the future.

STACEY CHOMIAK is an artist in the animation industry, getting her start on the well-loved series *My Little Pony: Friendship Is Magic*. She started out in graphic design, but followed her dream to work in animation and illustrate kids' books. Chomiak is a gay Christian, and loves to advocate and use her artistic talents for the LGBTQ Christian community. She and her wife, Tammy, live with their two young children and one cranky cat, nestled into the tall trees of the west coast of Canada.

When she isn't furiously sketching, Chomiak is likely to be out for a jog, critiquing her favorite film, or encouraging her children to dance with her.

8